Why is the Negro Lynched?

I0538147

BY THE LATE
FREDERICK DOUGLASS.

Reprinted by permission from "The A.M.E. Church Review" for Memorial Distribution, by a few of his English friends.

ISBN: 978-1-63923-749-4

Printed: February 2023

Published and Distributed By:
Lushena Books
607 Country Club Drive, Unit E
Bensenville, IL 60106
www.lushenabks.com

ISBN: 978-1-63923-749-4

We have felt that the most fitting tribute that we, of the Anti-Caste movement, can pay to the memory of this noble and faithful life is to issue broadcast -as far as the means entrusted to us will allow—his last great appeal for justice (uttered through the pages of " The A.M.E. Church Review only a few months before his death). A slanderous charge against Negro morality has gone forth throughout the world and has been widely credited. The white American has had his say both North and South. On behalf of the accused, Frederick Douglass claims, in the name of justice, to be heard.

Copies can be obtained free from the Editor of "Anti-Caste, Street, Somerset, England.

Why is the Negro Lynched?

("THE LESSON OF THE HOUR.")

BY THE LATE

FREDERICK DOUGLASS.

Reprinted by permission from the "A.M.E. Church Review."

I.

THE AFRO-AMERICAN PEOPLE INDICTED ON A NEW CHARGE.

INTRODUCTORY—THE WRITER'S CLAIM TO BE HEARD.*

I PROPOSE to give you a coloured man's view of the so-called "Negro Problem." We have had the Southern white man's view of this subject at large in the press, in the pulpit and on the platform. He has spoken in the pride of his power and to willing ears. Coloured by his peculiar environments, his version has been presented with abundant repetition, with startling emphasis, and with every advantage to his side of the question. We have also had the Northern white man's view of the subject, tempered by his distance from the scene and by his different, if not his higher, civilization. This quality and quantity of evidence, may be considered by some men as all sufficient upon which to found an intelligent judgment of the whole matter in controversy, and, therefore, it may be thought my testimony is not needed. But experience has taught us that it is sometimes wise and necessary to have more than two witnesses to bring out the whole truth. Especially is this the case where one of such witnesses has a powerful motive for suppressing or distorting the facts, as in this case. I therefore insist upon my right to take the witness stand and give my version of this Southern question, and though it shall widely differ from that of both the

---

* The headings and divisions are not in the original copy.

North and South, I shall submit the same to the candid judgment of all who hear me in full confidence that it will be received as true, by honest men and women of both sections of this Republic.

There is one thing, however, in which I think we must all agree at the start. It is that this so-called but mis-called Negro problem is one of the most important and urgent subjects that can now engage public attention. Its solution is, and ought to be, the serious business of the best American wisdom and statesmanship. For it involves the honour or dishonour, the glory or shame, the happiness or misery, of the whole American people. It not only touches the good name and fame of the Republic, but its highest moral welfare and its permanent safety. The evil with which it confronts us is coupled with a peril at once great and increasing, and one which should be removed, if it can be, without delay.

EPIDEMIC OF MOB-LAW.

The presence of eight millions of people in any section of this country, constituting an aggrieved class, smarting under terrible wrongs, denied the exercise of the commonest rights of humanity, and regarded by the ruling class of that section as outside of the government, outside of the law, outside of society, having nothing in common with the people with whom they live, the sport of mob violence and murder, is not only a disgrace and a scandal to that particular section, but a menace to the peace and security of the whole country. There is, as we all know, a perfect epidemic of mob law and persecution now pre-vailing at the South, and the indications of a speedy end are not hopeful. Great and terrible as have been its ravages in the past, it now seems to be increasing, not only in the number of its victims, but in its frantic rage and savage extravagance. Lawless vengeance is begin-ning to be visited upon white men as well as black. Our newspapers are daily disfigured by its ghastly horrors. It is no longer local but national ; no longer confined to the South but has invaded the North. The contagion is spreading, extending and overleaping geographical lines and state boundaries, and if permitted to go on, threatens to destroy all respect for law and order, not only in the South but in all parts of our common country, North as well as South. For certain it is, that crime allowed to go unpunished, unresisted and unarrested, will breed crime.

When the poison of anarchy is once in the air, like the pestilence that walketh in darkness, the winds of heaven will take it up and favour its diffusion. Though it may strike down the weak to-day, it will strike down the strong to-morrow.

Not a breeze comes to us from the late rebellious states that is not tainted and freighted with Negro blood. In its thirst for blood and its rage for vengeance, the mob has blindly, boldly and defiantly supplanted sheriffs, constables and police. It has assumed all the functions of civil authority. It laughs at legal processes, courts and juries, and its red-handed murderers range abroad unchecked and unchallenged by law or by public opinion. If the mob is in pursuit of Negroes who happen to be accused of crime, innocent or guilty, prison walls and iron bars afford no protection. Jail doors are battered down in the presence of unresisting jailors, and the accused, awaiting trial in the courts of law, are dragged out and hanged, shot, stabbed or burned to death, as the blind and irresponsible mob may elect.

We claim to be a highly-civilized and Christian country. I will not stop to deny this claim, yet I fearlessly affirm that there is nothing in the history of savages to surpass the blood-chilling horrors and fiendish excesses perpetrated against the coloured people of this country, by the so-called enlightened and Christian people of the South. It is commonly thought that only the lowest and most disgusting birds and beasts, such as buzzards, vultures and hyenas, will gloat over and prey upon dead bodies ; but the Southern mob, in its rage, feeds its vengeance by shooting, stabbing and burning their victims, when they are dead.

Now, what is the special charge by which this ferocity is justified, and by which mob law is excused and defended even by good men North and South ? It is a charge of recent origin ; a charge never brought before ; a charge never heard of in the time of slavery or in any other time in our history. It is a charge of assaults by Negroes upon white women. This new charge, once fairly started on the wings of rumour, no matter by whom or in what manner originated, whether well or ill-founded, whether true or false, is certain to raise a mob and to subject the accused to immediate torture and death. It is nothing that there may be a mistake in his case as to identity.

It is nothing that the victim pleads " not guilty." It is nothing that the accused is of fair reputation and his accuser is of an abandoned character. It is nothing that the majesty of the law is defied and insulted ; no time is allowed for defence or explanation ; he is bound with cords, hurried off amid the frantic yells and curses of the mob to the scaffold, and there, under its ghastly shadow, he is tortured, till by pain or promises, he is made to think that he can possibly gain time or save his life by confession—confesses—and then, whether guilty or innocent, he is shot, hanged, stabbed or burned to death amid the wild shouts of the mob. When the will of the mob is accomplished, when its thirst for blood has been quenched, when its victim is speechless, silent and dead, his mobocratic accusers and murderers of course have the ear of the world all to themselves, and the world, hearing only the testimony of the mob, generally approves its verdict.

Such, then, is the state of Southern law and civilization at this moment, in relation to the coloured citizens of that section of our country. Though the picture is dark and terrible, I venture to affirm that no man, North or South, can successfully deny its essential truth.

ATTITUDE OF UPPER CLASSES.

Now the question arises, and it is important to know, how this state of affairs is viewed by the better classes of the Southern States. I will tell you, and I venture to say in advance, if our hearts were not already hardened by familiarity with crimes against the Negro, we should be shocked and astonished, not only by these mobocratic crimes, but by the attitude of the better classes of the Southern people and their law-makers, towards the perpetrators of them. With a few noble exceptions, just enough to prove the rule, the upper classes of the South seem to be in full sympathy with the mob and its deeds. There are but few earnest words ever uttered against either. Press, platform and pulpit are generally either silent or they openly apologise for the mob and its deeds. The mobocratic murderers are not only permitted to go free, untried and unpunished, but are lauded and applauded as honourable men and good citizens, the high-minded guardians of Southern virtue. If lynch law is in any case condemned by them, it is only condemned in one breath and excused in another.

The great trouble with the Negro in the South is that all presumptions are against him. A white man has but to blacken his face and commit a crime to have some Negro lynched in his stead. An abandoned woman has only to start a cry, true or false, that she has been insulted by a black man, to have him arrested and summarily murdered by the mob. Frightened and tortured by his captors, confused, he may be, into telling crooked stories about his whereabouts at the time when the crime is alleged to have been committed, and the death penalty is at once inflicted, though his story may be but the incoherency of ignorance or the distraction caused by terror.

In confirmation of what I have said, I have before me the utterances of some of the best people of the South, and also the testimony of one from the North, a lady of high character, from whom, considering her antecedents, we should have expected a more considerate, just and humane utterance.

In a late number of the *Forum*, Bishop Haygood, author of the "Brother in Black," says that "The most alarming fact is that execution by lynching has ceased to surprise us. The burning of a human being for any crime, it is thought, is a horror that does not occur outside of the Southern states of the American Union, yet unless assaults by Negroes come to an end, there will most probably be still further display of vengeance that will shock the world, and men who are just will consider the provocation."

In an open letter addressed to me by ex-Governor Chamberlain, of South Carolina, published in the Charleston *News and Courier*, in reply to an article of mine on the subject of lynching, published in the *North American Review*, the ex-Governor says: "Your denunciation of the South on this point is directed exclusively, or nearly so, against the application of lynch law for the punishment of one crime; the existence, I suppose I might say the prevalence, of this crime at the South is undeniable. But I read your article in vain for any special denunciation of the crime itself. As you say, your people are lynched, tortured and burned, for assault on white women. As you value your own good fame and safety as a race, stamp out the infamous crime."

And now comes the sweet voice of a Northern woman,

Miss Frances Willard, of the W. C. T. U., distinguished among her sisters for benevolence and Christian charity. She speaks in the same bitter tone and hurls against us the same blasting accusation. She says in a letter now before me, " I pity the Southerners. The problem in their hands is immeasurable. The coloured race multiplies like the locusts of Egypt. The safety of women, of childhood, of the home, is menaced in a thousand localities at this moment, so that men dare not go beyond the sight of their own roof tree." Such, then, is the crushing indictment drawn up against the Southern Negroes, drawn up, too, by persons who are perhaps the fairest and most humane of the Negro's accusers. Yet even they paint him as a moral monster, ferociously invading the sacred rights of woman and endangering the homes of the whites.

INCRIMINATION OF THE WHOLE RACE.

Now, I hold, no less than his accusers, that the crime alleged against the Negro is the most revolting which men can commit. It is a crime that awakens the intensest abhorrence and tempts mankind to kill the criminal on first sight.

But this charge thus brought against the Negro and as constantly reiterated by his enemies, is plainly enough not merely a charge against the individual culprit, as would be the case with an individual of any other race, but it is in large measure a charge constructively against the coloured people as such. It throws over every man of colour a mantle of odium, and sets upon him a mark of popular hate, more distressing than the mark set upon the first murderer. It points the Negro out as an object of suspicion, avoidance and hate.

It is in this form of the charge that you and I and all of us are required to meet it and refute it, if that can be done. In the opinion of some of us it were well to say nothing about it, that the least said about it the better. They would have us suffer quietly under the odium in silence. In this I do not concur. Taking this charge in its broad and comprehensive sense, the sense in which it is presented and, as now stated, it strikes at the whole coloured race, and, therefore, as a coloured man, I am bound to meet it. I am grateful for the opportunity now afforded me to meet it. For I believe it can be met and met successfully. I hold that a people too spiritless to defend themselves against unjust imputations, are not worth defending, and are not worthy to defend anything else.

II.

THE DEFENCE—"NOT GUILTY."

CHARACTER OF THEIR ACCUSERS CHALLENGED.

Without boasting in advance, but relying upon the goodness of my cause, I will say here I am ready to confront Ex-Governor Chamberlain, Bishop Fitzgerald, Bishop Haygood and good Miss Frances Willard and all others, singly or altogether, who bring this charge against the coloured people as a class.

But I want however, to be clearly understood at the outset. I do not pretend that Negroes are saints and angels. I do not deny that they are capable of committing the crime imputed to them, but utterly deny that they are any more addicted to the commission of that crime than is true of any other variety of the human family. In entering upon my argument, I may be allowed to say again what should be taken for granted at the start, that I am not a defender of any man guilty of this atrocious crime, but a defender of the coloured people as a class.

In answer, then, to the terrible indictment thus read, and speaking for the coloured people as a class, I venture in their name and in their stead, here and now, to plead "not guilty," and shall submit my case with confidence of acquittal by good men and women, North and South, before whom we are, as a class, now being tried. In daring to do this I know that the moral atmosphere about me is not favourable to my cause. The sentiment left by slavery is still with us, and the moral vision of the American people is still darkened by its presence.

It is the misfortune of the coloured people of this country that the sins of the few are visited more or less upon the many. In respect to the offenders, I am with General Grant and every other honest man. My motto is, "Let no guilty man escape." But while I say this, and mean to say it strongly, I am also here to say, let no guilty man be condemned and killed by the mob, or crushed under the weight of a charge of which he is not guilty.

I need not be told that the cause I have undertaken to

support is not to be maintained by any mere confident assertions or general denials, however strongly worded. If I had no better ground to stand upon than this, I would at once leave the field of controversy and give up the coloured man's cause to his accusers. I am also aware that I am here to do in some measure what the masters of logic say is impossible to be done. I know that I cannot prove a negative; there is one thing that I can and will do. I will call in question the affirmative. I can and will show that there are sound reasons for doubting and denying this horrible charge of rape as the special and peculiar crime of the coloured people of the South. I doubt it, and deny it with all my soul. My doubt and denial are based upon three fundamental grounds.

The first ground is, the well-established and well-tested character of the Negro on the very point upon which he is now so violently and persistently accused. I contend that his whole history in bondage and out of bondage contradicts and gives the lie to the allegation. My second ground for doubt and denial is based upon what I know of the character and antecedents of the men and women who bring this charge against him. My third ground is the palpable unfitness of the mob to testify and which is the main witness in the case.

I therefore affirm that a fierce and frenzied mob is not and ought not to be deemed a competent witness against any man accused of any crime whatever, and especially the crime now in question. The ease with which a mob can be collected, the slight causes by which it can be set in motion, and the element of which it is composed, deprives its testimony of the qualities necessary to sound judgment and that which should inspire confidence and command belief. Blinded by its own fury, it is moved by impulses utterly unfavourable to a clear perception of facts and the ability to make an impartial statement of the simple truth. At the outset, I challenge the credibility of the mob, and as the mob is the main witness in the case against the Negro I appeal from the judgment of the mob to the judgment of law-abiding men, in support of my challenge. I lay special emphasis on the fact that it is the mob and the mob only that the country has recognised and accepted as its accredited witness against the Negro. The mob is its law, its judge, jury and executioner. I need not argue this point further. Its truth is borne upon its face.

But I go further. I dare not only to impeach the mob, I impeach and discredit the veracity of men generally, whether mobocrats or otherwise who sympathise with lynch law, whenever or wherever the acts of coloured men are in question. It seems impossible for such men to judge a coloured man fairly. I hold that men who openly and deliberately nullify the laws and violate the provisions of the Constitution of their country, which they have solemnly sworn to support and execute, are not entitled to unqualified belief in any case, and certainly not in the case of the Negro. I apply to them the legal maxim, "False in one, false in all." Especially do I apply this maxim when the conduct of the Negro is in question.

Again I question the Negro's accusers on another important ground; I have no confidence in the veracity of men who publicly justify themselves in cheating the Negro out of his constitutional right to vote. The men who do this, either by false returns, or by taking advantage of the Negro's illiteracy, or by surrounding the ballot box with obstacles and sinuosities intended to bewilder him and defeat his rightful exercise of the elective franchise, are men who should not be believed on oath. That this is done and approved in Southern States is notorious. It has been openly defended by so-called honest men inside and outside of Congress.

I met this shameless defence of crime face to face at the late Chicago Auxiliary Congress, during the World's Columbian Exposition, in a solemn paper by Prof. Weeks, of North Carolina, who boldly advocated this kind of fraud as necessary and justifiable in order to secure Anglo-Saxon supremacy, and in doing so, as I believe, he voiced the moral sentiment of Southern men generally.

Now, men who openly defraud the Negro of his vote by all manner of artifice, who justify it and boast of it in the face of the world's civilization, as was done by Prof. Weeks at Chicago, I hardly need say that such men are not to be depended upon for truth in any case where the rights of the Negro are involved. Their testimony in the case of any other people than the Negro would be instantly and utterly discredited, and why not the same in this case? Every honest man will see that this point is well taken. It has for its support common sense, common honesty, and the best sentiment of mankind. On the other hand, it has nothing to oppose it but a vulgar, popular prejudice against the coloured people of our country, a prejudice which we all know strikes men with moral blindness and renders them incapable of seeing any distinction between right and wrong where coloured people are concerned.

THE NEGRO'S CLEAN RECORD DURING WAR TIME.

But I come to a stronger position. I rest my denial not merely upon general principles but upon well-known facts. I reject the charge brought against the Negro as a class, because all through the late war, while the slave-masters of the South were absent from their homes, in the field of rebellion, with bullets in their pockets, treason in their hearts, broad blades in their bloody hands, seeking the life of the nation, with the vile purpose of perpetuating the enslavement of the Negro, their wives, their daughters, their sisters and their mothers were left in the absolute custody of these same Negroes, and during all those long four years of terrible conflict, when the Negro had every opportunity to commit the abominable crime now alleged against him, there was never a single instance of such crime reported or charged against him. He was never accused of assault, insult, or an attempt to commit an assault upon any white woman in the whole South. A fact like this, though negative, speaks volumes, and ought to have some weight with the American people on the present question.

Then, again, on general principles, I do not believe the charge, because it implies an improbable change, if not an impossible change in the mental and moral character and composition of the Negro. It implies a radical change wholly inconsistent with the well-known facts of human nature. It is a contradiction to human experience. History does not present an example of a transformation in the character of any class of men so extreme, so unnatural and so complete as is implied in this charge. The change is too great and the period for it too brief. Instances may be cited where men fall like stars from heaven, but such is not the usual experience with the masses. Decline in the moral character of such is not sudden, but gradual. The downward steps are marked at first by slow degrees and by increasing momentum, going from bad to worse as they proceed. Time is an element in such changes, and I contend that the Negroes of the South have not had time to experience this great change and reach this lower depth of infamy. On the contrary, in point of fact, they have been, and still are, improving and ascending to higher and still higher levels of moral and social worth.

EXCUSES FOR LYNCHING—DELICACY OF SUBJECT ;

POSSIBILITY OF CRIMINAL'S ESCAPE FROM JUSTICE.

Again I utterly deny the charge on the fundamental ground that those who bring the charge do not and dare not give the Negro a chance to be heard in his own defence. He is not allowed to show the deceptive conditions out of which the charge has originated. He is not allowed to vindicate his own character from blame, or to criminate the character and motives of his accusers. Even the mobocrats themselves admit that it would be fatal to their purpose to have the character of the Negro's accusers brought into court. They pretend to a delicate regard for the feelings of the parties alleged to have been assaulted. They are too modest to have them brought into court. They are, therefore, for lynching and against giving a fair trial to the accused. This excuse, it is needless to say, is contemptible and hypocritical. It is not only mock modesty, but mob modesty. Men who can collect hundreds and thousands of their kind, if we believe them, thirsting for vengeance, and can spread before them in the tempest and whirlwind of vulgar passion, the most disgusting details of crime, connecting the names of women with the same, should not be allowed to shelter themselves under any pretence of modesty. Such a pretence is absurd and shameless upon the face of it. Who does not know that the modesty of womanhood is always and in every such case an object for special protection in a court of law ? On the other hand, who does not know that a lawless mob, composed in part of the basest men, can have no such respect for the modesty of women, as has a court of law. No woman need be ashamed to confront one who has insulted or assaulted her in any court of law. Besides, innocence does not hesitate to come to the rescue of justice, and need not even in this case.

Again, I do not believe it, and deny it because if the evidence were deemed sufficient to bring the accused to the scaffold by a verdict of an impartial jury, there could be and would be no objection to having the alleged offender tried in conformity to due process of law.

The only excuse for lynch law, which has a shadow of support in it is, that the criminal would probably otherwise be allowed to escape the punishment due to his crime. But this excuse is not employed by the lynchers, though it is sometimes so employed by those who apologise for the lynchers. But for it there is no foundation whatever, in a country like the South, where public opinion, the laws, the courts, the juries, the advocates, are all against the Negro, especially one alleged to be guilty of the crime now charged. That such an one would be permitted to escape condign punishment, is not only untenable but an insult to common sense. The chances are that not even an innocent Negro so charged would be allowed to escape.

III.

THE THREE STAGES OF NEGRO PERSECUTION.

THEIR OBJECT—HIS DISFRANCHISEMENT.

But I come to another fact, and an all important fact, bearing upon this case. You will remember that during all the first years of reconstruction, and long after the war, Negroes were slain by scores. The world was shocked by these murders, so that the Southern press and people found it necessary to invent, adopt and propagate almost every species of falsehood to create sympathy for themselves, and to formulate excuses for thus gratifying their brutal instincts against the Negro ; there was never at that time a charge made against any Negro involving an assault upon any white woman or upon little white children in all the South. During all this time the white women and children were absolutely safe. During all this time there was no call for Miss Willard's pity, or for Bishop Haygood's defence of burning Negroes to death, but killing Negroes went on all the same.

You will remember also that during this time the justification for the murder of Negroes was said to be Negro conspiracies, Negro insurrections, Negro schemes to murder all the white people, Negro plots to burn the town and to commit violence generally. These were the excuses then depended upon, but never a word was then said or whispered about Negro outrages upon white women and children. So far as the history of that time is concerned, white women and children were absolutely safe, and husbands and fathers could leave their homes without the slightest anxiety for the safety of their families. But now mark the change and the reasons for the change. When events proved that no such conspiracies, no such insurrections as were then pretended to exist, and which were then paraded before the world in glaring headlines in the columns of nearly all our newspapers, had ever existed or were even meditated— when these excuses had run their course and had served their wicked purpose, when the huts of the Negroes had been searched, and searched in vain for guns and ammunition to prove these charges against the Negro, and no such proof was found, when there was no way open thereafter to prove these charges against the Negro, and no way to make the North believe in them, they did not even then bring forward the present allegation, but went on harassing and killing Negroes just the same. But this time they based their right to kill on the ground that it was necessary to check the domination and supremacy of the Negro and to secure the absolute rule of the Anglo-Saxon race.

It is important to notice and emphasize here the significant fact that there has been three distinct periods of persecutions of the Negroes in the South, and three distinct sets of excuses for this persecution. They have come along precisely in the order they were most needed. Each was made to fit its special place. First, you remember, as I have said, it was insurrection. When that wore out, Negro supremacy became the excuse. When that was worn out, then came the charge of assault upon defenceless women. I undertake to say that this orderly arrangement and periodicity of excuses are significant. They mean something, and should not be overlooked. They show design, plan, purpose and invention. And now that Negro insurrection and Negro domination are no longer defensible as an excuse for Negro persecution, there has come in due course another suited to the occasion, and that is the heart-rending cry of the white women and little white children.

Now, my friends, I ask what is the manifest meaning of

this charge at this time? What is the meaning of the singular omission of this charge during the two periods preceding the present? Why was not this charge made at that time as now? The Negro was the same man then as to-day. Why, I ask again, was not this dreadful charge brought forward against the Negro in war times and in reconstruction times? Had it existed either in war times or during reconstruction, does any man doubt that it would have been added to the other charges and proclaimed upon the house-tops and at the street corners, as this charge is at present?

I will answer the question: or you yourselves have already given the true answer. For the plain and only rational explanation is that there was at the times specified no foundation for such a charge, or that the charge itself was either not thought of, or if thought of it was not deemed necessary to excuse the lawless violence with which the Negro was then pursued and killed. The old charges already enumerated were deemed all sufficient.

Things have changed since then, and the old excuses are not now available. The times have changed, and the Negro's accusers have found it necessary to change with them. They have been compelled to invent a new charge to suit the times. The old charges are no longer valid. Upon them the good opinion of the North and of mankind cannot be secured. Honest men no longer believe that there is any ground to apprehend Negro supremacy. Times and events have swept away these old refuges of lies. They were once powerful. They did their work in their day and did it with terrible energy and effect, but they are now cast aside as useless. The lie has lost its ability to deceive. The altered times and circumstances have made necessary a sterner, stronger and more effective justification of Southern barbarism, and hence we have, according to my theory, to look into the face of a more shocking and blasting charge than either Negro supremacy or Negro insurrection.

I insist upon it that this new charge has come at the call of new conditions, and that nothing could have been hit upon better calculated to accomplish its brutal purpose. It clouds the character of the Negro with a crime the most shocking that men can commit, and is fitted to drive from the criminal all pity and all fair play and all mercy. It is a crime that places him outside of the pale of the law, and settles upon his shoulders a mantle of wrath and fire, that blisters and burns into his very soul.

It is for this purpose, it seems to me, that this new charge, unthought of and unknown in the times to which I have referred, has been largely invented and thundered against us. It is for this purpose that it has been constantly reiterated and adopted. It was intended to blast and ruin the Negro's character as a man and a citizen. I need not tell you how thoroughly it has already done its work. The Negro may and does feel its malign influence in the very air he breathes. He may read it in the faces of men among whom he moves. It has cooled his friends; it has heated his enemies and arrested at home and abroad, in some measure, the generous efforts that good men were wont to make for his improvement and elevation. It has deceived his friends at the North and many good friends at the South, for nearly all of them, in some measure, have accepted this charge against the Negro as true. Its perpetual reiteration in our newspapers and magazines has led men and women to regard him with averted eyes, dark suspicion and increasing hate.

Some of the Southern papers have denounced me for my unbelief in this charge and in this new crusade against the Negro, but I repeat I do not believe it, and firmly deny the grounds upon which it is based. I reject it because I see in it evidence of an invention called into being by a well-defined motive, a motive sufficient to stamp it as a gross expedient to justify murderous assault upon a long enslaved and hence a hated people.

I not only reject it because it bears upon its face the marks of being a fraud, a make-shift for a malignant purpose, but because it has sprung upon the country simultaneously, and in manifest co-operation with a declared purpose and a well-known effort, and I may say a .fixed determination to degrade the Negro by judicial decisions, by legislative enactments, by repealing all laws for the protection of the ballot, by drawing the colour line in all railroad cars and stations and in all other public places in the South, thus to pave the way to a final consummation which is nothing less than the Negro's entire disenfranchisement as an American citizen. It is to this great end that all the charges and complaints against the Negro are directed and are made to converge. This is and has been from first to last the grand and all-commanding object in view. It is a part of a well-devised reactionary movement against the Negro as a citizen. The old master class are wise in their day and generation. They know if they can once divest the Negro of the elective franchise and nullify his citizenship, the partition wall between him and slavery will no longer exist, and no man can tell where the reaction will stop.

THE ATTACK LESS UPON CRIME THAN COLOUR.

Again, I do not believe it, and deny it, because the charge is not so much against the crime itself, as against the colour of the people alleged to be guilty of it. Slavery itself, you will remember, was a system of unmitigated, legalised outrage upon black women of the South, and no white man was ever shot, burned or hanged for availing himself of all the power that slavery gave him at this point.

To sum up my argument on this lynching business, it remains to be said that I have shown that the Negro's accusers in this case have violated their oaths, and have cheated the Negro out of his vote ; that they have robbed and defrauded the Negro systematically and persistently, and have boasted of it. I have shown that when the Negro had every opportunity to commit the crime now charged against him, he was never accused of it by his bitterest enemies. I have shown that during all the years of reconstruction, when he was being murdered at Hamburg, Yazoo, New Orleans, Copiah and elsewhere, he was never accused at that time of the crime now charged against him. I have shown that in the nature of things no such change in the character and composition of a whole people, as this implies, could have taken place within the limited period allowed for it. I have shown that those who accuse him dare not confront him in a court of law and have their witnesses subjected to proper legal inquiry. I have shown from the very constitution of a mob, the slight causes by which it may be created, and the sentiment by which it is impelled, it cannot be depended upon for either truth or justice. I have shown that its sole aim is to execute, not to find a true verdict. And showing all this and more, I have shown that they who

charge the Negro with this foul crime, in such
circumstances, may be justly doubted and deemed
unworthy of belief.

IV.

OBJECTIONS ANSWERED: PECULIARITIES OF SOUTHERN
SENTIMENT. LACK OF RESPECT FOR HUMAN LIFE.

But I now come to a grave objection to my theory of
this violent persecution. I shall be told by many of my
Northern friends that my argument, though plausible, is
not conclusive. It will be said that the charges against
the Negro are specific and positive, and that there must
be some foundation for them, because, as they allege, men
in their normal condition do not shoot, hang and burn
their fellow men who are guiltless of crime. Well! This
assumption is very just and very charitable. I only wish
that something like the same justice and the same charity
shall be shown to the Negro. All credit is due and is
accorded to our Northern friends for their humane
judgment of the South. Humane themselves, they are
slow to believe that the mobocrats are less humane
than themselves. Their hearts are right but their heads are
wrong. They apply a general rule to a special case.
They forget that neither the mob nor its victims are in a
normal condition. Both are exceptions to the general
rule. The force of the argument against my version of
the case is the assumption that the lynchers are like
other men and that the Negro has the same hold on the
protection of society that other men have. Neither
assumption is true. The lynchers and mobocrats are not
like other men, nor is the Negro hedged about by the
same protection accorded other members of society.

The point I make, then, is this. That I am not, in this
case, dealing with men in their natural condition. I am
dealing with men brought up in the exercise of
irresponsible power. I am dealing with men whose ideas,
habits and customs are entirely different from those of
ordinary men. It is, therefore, quite gratuitous to assume
that the principles that apply to other men, apply to the
lynchers and murderers of the Negro. The rules resting
upon the justice and benevolence of human nature do not
apply to the mobocrats, or to those who were educated in
the habits and customs of a slave-holding community.
What these habits are I have a right to know, both in

theory and practice. Whoever has read the laws of the late slave states relating to the Negroes, will see what I mean.

I repeat, the mistake made by those who, on this ground, object to my theory of the charge against the Negro, is that they overlook the natural influence of the life, education and habits of the lynchers. We must remember that these people have not now and have never had any such respect for human life as is common to other men. They have had among them for centuries a peculiar institution, and that peculiar institution has stamped them as a peculiar people. They were not before the war, they were not during the war, and have not been since the war, in their spirit or in their civilization, a people in common with the people of the North, or the civilized world. I will not here harrow up your feelings by detailing their treatment of Northern prisoners during the war. Their institutions have taught them no respect for human life, and especially the life of the Negro. It has, in fact, taught them absolute contempt for his life. The sacredness of life which ordinary men feel does not touch them anywhere. A dead Negro is with them now, as before, a common jest.

They care no more for the Negro's rights to live than they care for his rights to liberty, or his right to the ballot or any other right. Chief Justice Taney told the exact truth about these people when he said : "They did not consider that the black man had any rights which white men were bound to respect." No man of the South ever called in question that statement, and no man ever will. They could always shoot, stab, hang and burn the Negro, without any such remorse or shame as other men would feel after committing such a crime. Any Southern man, who is honest and is frank enough to talk on the subject, will tell you that he has no such idea as we have of the sacredness of human rights, and especially, as I have said, of the life of the Negro. Hence it is absurd to meet my arguments with the facts predicated of our common human nature.

I know that I shall be charged with apologising for criminals. Ex-Governor Chamberlain has already virtually done as much. But there is no foundation for such charge. I affirm that neither I nor any other coloured man of like standing with myself has ever raised a finger or uttered a word in defence of any man, black or white, known to be guilty of the dreadful crime now in question.

But what I contend for, and what every honest man, black or white, has a right to contend for, is that when any man is accused of this or any other crime, of whatever name, nature, degree or extent, he shall have the benefit of a legal investigation; that he shall be confronted by his accusers; and that he shall, through proper counsel, be allowed to question his accusers in open court and in open daylight, so that his guilt or his innocence may be duly proved and established.

If this is to make me liable to the charge of apologising for crime, I am not ashamed to be so charged. I dare to contend for the coloured people of the United States that they are a law-abiding people, and I dare to insist upon it that they or any other people, black or white, accused of crime, shall have a fair trial before they are punished.

GENERAL UNFAIRNESS—THE CHICAGO EXHIBITION, ETC.

Again, I cannot dwell too much upon the fact that coloured people are much damaged by this charge. As an injured class we have a right to appeal from the judgment of the mob, to the judgment of the law and to the justice of the American people.

Full well our enemies have known where to strike and how to stab us most fatally. Owing to popular prejudice, it has become the misfortune of the coloured people of the South and of the North as well, to have, as I have said, the sins of the few visited upon the many.

When a white man steals, robs or murders, his crime is visited upon his own head alone. But not so with the black man. When he commits a crime, the whole race is made responsible. The case before us is an example. This unfairness confronts us not only here but it confronts us everywhere else.

Even when American art undertakes to picture the types of the two races, it invariably places in comparison, not the best of both races as common fairness would dictate, but it puts side by side and in glaring contrast, the lowest type of the Negro with the highest type of the white man and then calls upon the world to " look upon this picture, then upon that."

When a black man's language is quoted, in order to belittle and degrade him, his ideas are often put in the most grotesque and unreadable English, while the utterances of Negro scholars and authors are ignored. To-day, Sojourner Truth is more readily quoted than Alexander Cromwell or Dr. James McCune Smith. A hundred white men will attend a concert of counterfeit Negro minstrels, with faces blackened with burnt cork, to one who will attend a lecture by an intelligent Negro.

Even the late World's Columbian Exposition was guilty of this unfairness. While I join with all other men in pronouncing the Exposition itself one of the grandest demonstrations of civilization that the world has ever seen, yet great and glorious as it was, it was made to show just this kind of injustice and discrimination against the Negro.

As nowhere in the world, it was hoped that here the idea of human brotherhood would have been grandly recognized and most gloriously illustrated. It should have been thus and would have been thus, had it been what it professed to be, a World's Exposition. It was not such, however, in its spirit at this point; it was only an American Exposition. The spirit of American caste against the educated Negro was conspicuously seen from start to finish, and to this extent the Exposition was made simply an American Exposition instead of a World's Exposition.

Since the day of Pentecost there was never assembled in any one place or on any one occasion a larger variety of peoples of all forms, features and colors and all degrees of civilization, than was assembled at this World's Exposition. It was a grand ethnological object lesson, a fine chance to study all likenesses and all differences of mankind. Here were Japanese, Soudanese, Chinese, Singalese, Syrians Persians, Tunisians, Algerians, Egyptians, East Indians, Laplanders, Esquimaux, and, as if to shame the educated Negro of America, the Dahomeyans were there to exhibit their barbarism and increase American contempt for the Negro intellect. All classes and conditions were there save the educated American Negro. He ought to have been there, if only to show what American slavery and American freedom have done for him. The fact that all other nations were there at their best, made the Negro's exclusion the more pronounced and the more significant. People from abroad noticed the fact that while we have eight millions of colored people in the United States, many of them gentlemen and scholars, not one of them was deemed worthy to be appointed a Commissioner, or a member of an important committee, or a guide or a guard on the Exposition grounds, and this was evidently an intentional slight to the race. What a commentary is this upon the liberality of our boasted American liberty and American equality! It is a silent example, to be sure, but it is one that speaks louder than words. It says to the world that the colored people of America are not deemed by Americans as within the compass of American law, progress and civilization. It says to the lynchers and mobocrats of the South, go on in your hellish work of Negro persecution. You kill their bodies, we kill their souls.

V.

NEGRO SUFFRAGE : ATTEMPT TO ABRIDGE THE RIGHT.

THE LOWLY NEED ITS PROTECTION.

But now a word on the question of Negro suffrage. It has come to be fashionable of late to ascribe much of the trouble at the South to ignorant Negro suffrage. That great measure recommended by General Grant and adopted by the loyal nation, is now denounced as a blunder and a failure. The proposition now is, therefore, to find some way to abridge and limit this right by imposing upon it an educational or some other qualification. Among those who take this view of the question are Mr. John J. Ingalls and Mr. John M. Langston, one white and the other colored. They are both distinguished leaders ; the one is the leader of the whites and the other is the leader of the blacks. They are both eloquent, both able, and both wrong. Though they are both Johns, neither of them is to my mind a "St. John," and not even a "John the Baptist." They have taken up an idea which they seem to think quite new, but which in reality is as old as despotism, and about as narrow and selfish as despotism. It has been heard and answered a thousand times over. It is the argument of the crowned heads and privileged classes of the world. It is as good against our Republican form of government as it is against the Negro. The wonder is that its votaries do not see its consequences. It does away with that noble and just idea of Abraham Lincoln that our government should be a government of the people, by the people and for the people and for *all* the people.

These gentlemen are very learned, very eloquent and very able, but I cannot follow them in this effort to restrict voting to the educated classes. Much learning has made them mad. Education is great but manhood is greater. The one is the principle, the other the accident. Man was not made as an attribute to education, but education as an attribute to man. I say to these gentlemen, first protect the man and you will thereby protect education. Do not make illiteracy a bar to the ballot, but make the ballot a bar to illiteracy. Take the ballot from the Negro and you take from him the means and motives that make for education. Those who are already educated and are vested with political power have thereby an advantage which they are not likely to divide with the Negro, especially when they have a fixed purpose to make this entirely a white man's government. I cannot, therefore, follow these gentlemen in a path so dangerous to the Negro. I would not make suffrage more exclusive but more inclusive. I would not have it embrace only the élite, but I would have it include the lowly. I would not only include the men, but would gladly include the women, and make our government in reality, as in name, a government by the people, of the people, and for the whole people.

But, manifestly, it is all nonsense to make suffrage to the coloured people, the cause of the failure of good government in the Southern states. On the contrary it is the lawless limitation of suffrage that makes the trouble.

Much thoughtless speech is heard about the ignorance of the Negro in the South. But plainly enough, it is not the ignorance of the Negro but the malevolence of his accusers, which is the real cause of Southern disorder. It is easy to show that the illiteracy of the Negro has no part or lot in the disturbances there. They who contend for disfranchisement on this ground, know, and know very well, that there is no truth whatever in their contention. To make out their case, they must show that some oppressive and hurtful measure has been imposed upon the country by Negro voters. But they cannot show any such thing and they know it.

The Negro has never set up a separate party, never adopted a Negro platform, never proclaimed or adopted a separate policy for himself or for the country. His assailants know this and know that he has never acted apart from the whole American people. They know that he has never sought to lead, but has always been content to follow. They know that he has not made his ignorance the rule of his political conduct, but he has been guided by the rule of white men. They know that he simply kept pace with the average intelligence of his age and country. They know that he has gone steadily along in the line of his politics with the most enlightened citizens of the country and that he has never gone faster or farther. They know that he has always voted with one or the other of the two great political parties. They know that if the votes of these parties have been guided by intelligence and patriotism, the same must be said of the vote of the Negro. Knowing all this, they ought to know also, that it is a shame and an outrage upon common sense and fair dealing to hold him or his suffrage responsible for any disorder that may reign in the Southern States. Yet while any lie may be safely told against the Negro and will be credited by popular prejudice, this lie will find eloquent tongues, bold and shameless enough to tell it.

It is true that the Negro once voted solidly for the candidates of the republican party; but what if he did? He then only voted with John Mercer Langston, John J. Ingalls, John Sherman, General Harrison, Senator Hoar, Henry Cabot Lodge and Governor McKinley and many of the most intelligent statesmen and noblest patriots of whom this country can boast. The charge against him at this time is, therefore, utterly groundless and is used for fraud, violence and persecution.

The proposition to disfranchise the coloured voter of the South in order to solve the race problem, I therefore denounce as a false and cowardly proposition, utterly unworthy of an honest and grateful nation. It is a proposition to sacrifice friends in order to conciliate enemies; to surrender the constitution for the lack of moral courage to execute its provisions. It is a proclamation of the helplessness of the Nation to protect its own citizens. It says to the coloured citizen, " We cannot protect you, we therefore propose to join your oppressors. Your suffrage has been rendered a failure by violence, and we now propose to make it a failure by law."

Than this, there was never a surrender more dishonorable, more ungrateful, or more cowardly. Any statesman, black or white, who dares to support such a scheme by any concession, deserves no worse punishment than to be allowed to stay at home, deprived of all legislative trusts until he repents. Even then he should only be received on probation.

DECADENCE OF THE SPIRIT OF LIBERTY.

Do not ask me what will be the final result of the so-called Negro problem. I cannot tell you. I have sometimes thought that the American people are too great to be small, too just and magnanimous to oppress the weak, too brave to yield up the right to the strong, and too grateful for public services ever to forget them or to reward them. I have fondly hoped that this estimate of American character would soon cease to be contradicted or put in doubt. But events have made me doubtful. The favour with which this proposition of disfranchisement has been received by public men, white and black, by republicans as well as democrats, has shaken my faith in the nobility of the nation. I hope and trust all will come out right in the end, but the immediate future looks dark and troubled. I cannot shut my eyes to the ugly facts before me.

Strange things have happened of late and are still happening. Some of these tend to dim the lustre of the American name, and chill the hopes once entertained for the cause of American liberty. He is a wiser man than I am who can tell how low the moral sentiment of the Republic may yet fall. When the moral sense of a nation begins to decline, and the wheels of progress to roll backward, there is no telling how low the one will fall or where the other will stop. The downward tendency, already manifest, has swept away some of the most important safeguards of justice and liberty. The Supreme Court, has, in a measure, surrendered. State sovereignty is essentially restored. The Civil Rights Bill is impaired. The Republican party is converted into a party of money, rather than a party of humanity and justice. We may well ask, what next?

The pit of hell is said to be bottomless. Principles which we all thought to have been firmly and permanently settled by the late war have been boldly assaulted and overthrown by the defeated party. Rebel rule is now nearly complete in many states, and it is gradually capturing the nation's Congress. The cause lost in the war is the cause regained in peace, and the cause gained in war is the cause lost in peace.

There was a threat made long ago by an American statesman that the whole body of legislation enacted for the protection of American liberty and to secure the results of the war for the Union, should be blotted from the national statute bock. That threat is now being sternly pursued and may yet be fully realised. The repeal of the laws intended to protect the elective franchise has heightened the suspicion that Southern rule may yet become complete, though, I trust, not permanent. There is no denying that the trend is in the wrong direction at present. The late election, however, gives us hope that the loyal Republican party may yet return to its first love.

VI.

DELUSIVE COLONISATION SCHEMES.

But I now come to another proposition, held up as a solution of the race problem, and this I consider equally unworthy with the one just disposed of. The two belong to the same low-bred family of ideas.

It is the proposition to colonize the coloured people of America in Africa, or somewhere else. Happily this scheme will be defeated, both by its impolicy and its impracticability. It is all nonsense to talk about the removal of eight millions of the American people from their homes in America to Africa. The expense and hardships, to say nothing of the cruelty attending such a measure, would make success impossible. The American people are wicked, but they are not fools ; they will hardly be disposed to incur the expense, to say nothing of the injustice which this measure demands. Nevertheless, this colonizing scheme, unworthy as it is of American statesmanship, and American honour, and though full of mischief to the coloured people, seems to have a strong hold on the public mind, and at times has shown much life and vigor.

The bad thing about it is, that it has, of late, owing to persecution, begun to be advocated by coloured men of acknowledged ability and learning, and every little while some white statesman becomes its advocate. Those gentlemen will doubtless have their opinion of me; I certainly have mine of them. My opinion is, that if they are sensible, they are insincere; and if they are sincere, they are not sensible. They know, or they ought to know that it would take more money than the cost of the late war, to transport even one half of the coloured people of the United States to Africa. Whether intentionally or not, they are, as I think, simply trifling with an afflicted people. They urge them to look for relief where they ought to know that relief is impossible. The only excuse they can make for the measure is that there is no hope for the Negro here, and that the coloured people in America owe something to Africa.

This last sentimental idea makes colonization very fascinating to the dreamers of both colours. But there is really no foundation for it.

They tell us that we owe something to our native land. This sounds well. But when the fact is brought to view, which should never be forgotten, that a man can only have one native land and that is the land in which he is born, the bottom falls entirely out of this sentimental argument.

Africa, according to her colonization advocates, is by no means modest in her demands upon us. She calls upon us to send her only our best men. She does not want our riff-raff, but our best men. But these are just the men who are valuable and who are wanted at home. It is true that we have a few preachers and laymen with a missionary turn of mind whom we might easily spare. Some who would possibly do as much good by going there as by staying here. By this is not the colonization idea. Its advocates want not only the best, but millions of the best. Better still, they want the United States Government to vote the money to send them there. They do not seem to see that if the Government votes money to send the Negro to Africa, that the Government may employ means to complete the arrangement and compel us to go.

Now I hold that the American Negro owes no more to the Negroes in Africa than he owes to the Negroes in America. There are millions of needy people over there, but there are also millions of needy people over here as well, and the millions in America need intelligent men of their number to help them, as much as intelligent men are needed in Africa to help her people. Besides, we have a fight on our hands right here, a fight for the redemption of the whole race, and a blow struck successfully for the Negro in America, is a blow struck for the Negro in Africa. For, until the Negro is respected in America, he need not expect consideration elsewhere. All this native land talk, however, is nonsense. The native land of the American Negro is America. His bones, his muscles, his sinews, are all American. His ancestors for two hundred and seventy years have lived and laboured and died, on American soil, and millions of his posterity have inherited Caucasian blood.

It is pertinent, therefore, to ask, in view of this admixture, as well as in view of other facts, where the people of this mixed race are to go, for their ancestors are white and black, and it will be difficult to find their native land anywhere outside of the United States.

But the worst thing, perhaps, about this colonization nonsense is, that it tends to throw over the Negro a mantle of despair. It leads him to doubt the possibility of his progress as an American citizen. It also encourages popular prejudice with the hope that by persecution or by persuasion, the Negro can finally be dislodged and driven from his natural home, while in the nature of the case he must stay here and will stay here, if for no other reason than because he cannot well get away.

I object to the colonization scheme, because it tends to weaken the Negro's hold on one country, while it can give him no rational hope of another. Its tendency is to make him despondent and doubtful, where he should feel assured and confident. It forces upon him the idea that he is for ever doomed to be a stranger and a sojourner in the land of his birth, and that he has no permanent abiding place here.

All this is hurtful; with such ideas constantly flaunted before him, he cannot easily set himself to work to better his condition in such ways as are open to him here. It sets him to groping everlastingly after the impossible.

Every man who thinks at all, must know that home is the fountain head, the inspiration, the foundation and main support, not only of all social virtue but of all motives to human progress, and that no people can prosper, or amount to much, unless they have a home, or the hope of a home. A man who has not such an object, either in possession or in prospect, is a nobody and will never be anything else. To have a home, the Negro must have a country, and he is an enemy to the moral progress of the Negro, whether he knows it or not, who calls upon him to break up his home in this country, for an uncertain home in Africa.

But the agitation on this subject has a darker side still. It has already been given out that if we do not go of our own accord, we may be forced to go, at the point of the bayonet. I cannot say that we shall not have to face this hardship, but badly as I think of the tendency of our times, I do not think that American sentiment will ever reach a condition which will make the expulsion of the Negro from the United States by any such means, possible.

Yet, the way to make it possible is to predict it. There are people in the world who know how to bring their own prophecies to pass. The best way to get up a mob, is to say there will be one, and this is what is being done. Colonization is no solution, but an evasion. It is not repentance but putting the wronged ones out of our presence. It is not atonement, but banishment. It is not love, but hate. Its reiteration and agitation only serves to fan the flame of popular prejudice and to add insult to to injury.

The righteous judgment of mankind will say if the American people could endure the Negro's presence while a slave, they certainly can and ought to endure his presence as a free man.

If they could tolerate him when he was a heathen, they might bear with him now that he is a Christian. If they could bear with him when ignorant and degraded, they should bear with him now that he is a gentleman and a scholar.

But even the Southern whites have an interest in this question. Woe to the South when it no longer has the strong arm of the Negro to till its soil, " and woe to the nation when it shall employ the sword to drive the Negro from his native land."

Such a crime against justice, such a crime against gratitude, should it ever be attempted, would certainly bring a national punishment which would cause the earth to shudder. It would bring a stain upon the nation's honour, like the blood on Lady Macbeth's hand. The waters of all the oceans would not suffice to wash out the infamy. But the nation will commit no such crime. But in regard to this point of our future, my mind is easy. We are here and are here to stay. It is well for us and well for the American people to rest up on this as final.

EMANCIPATION CRIPPLED. LANDLORD AND TENANT.

Another mode of impeaching the wisdom of emancipation, and the one which seems to give special pleasure to our enemies, is, as they say, that the condition of the coloured people of the South has been made worse by emancipation.

The champions of this idea are the only men who glory in the good old times when the slaves were under the lash and were bought and sold in the market with horses, sheep, and swine. It is another way of saying that slavery is better than freedom ; that darkness is better than light, and that wrong is better than right ; that hell is better than heaven ! It is the American method of reasoning in all matters concerning the Negro. It inverts everything ; turns truth upside down, and puts the case of the unfortunate Negro inside out and wrong end foremost every time. There is, however, nearly always some truth on their side of error, and it is so in this case.

When these false reasoners assert that the condition of the emancipated slave is wretched and deplorable, they partly tell the truth, and I agree with them. I even concur with them in the statement that the Negro is physically, in certain localities, in a worse condition to-day than in the time of slavery, but I part with these gentlemen when they ascribe this condition to emancipation.

To my mind the blame does not rest upon emancipation, but the defeat of emancipation. It is not the work of the spirit of liberty, but the work of the spirit of bondage. It comes of the determination of slavery to perpetuate itself, if not under one form, then under another. It is due to the folly of endeavouring to put the new wine of liberty in the old bottles of slavery. I concede the evil, but deny the alleged cause.

The landowners of the South want the labour of the Negro on the hardest terms possible. They once had it for nothing. They now want it for next to nothing. To accomplish this, they have contrived three ways. The first is, to rent their land to the Negro at an exorbitant price per annum and compel him to mortgage his crop in advance to pay this rent. The laws under which this is done are entirely in the interest of the landlord. He has a first claim upon everything produced on the land. The Negro can have nothing, can keep nothing, can sell nothing, without the consent of the landlord. As the Negro is at the start poor and empty-handed, he has had to draw on the landlord for meat and bread to feed himself and family while his crop is growing. The landlord keeps books; the Negro does not; hence, no matter how hard he may work or how hard saving he may be, he is, in most cases, brought in debt at the end of the year, and once in debt he is fastened to the land as by hooks of steel. If he attempts to leave he may be arrested under the order of the law.

Another way, which is still more effective, is the practice of paying the labourer with orders on the store instead of lawful money. By this means money is kept out of the hands of the Negro, and the Negro is kept entirely in the hands of the landlord. He cannot save money because he gets no money to save. He cannot seek a better market for his labour because he has no money with which to pay his fare, and because he is, by that vicious order system, already in debt, and therefore already in bondage. Thus he is riveted to one place, and is, in some sense, a slave; for a man to whom it can be said, "You shall work for me for what I choose to pay you, and how I shall choose to pay you," is, in fact, a slave, though he may be called a free man.

We denounce the landlord and tenant system of England, but it can be said of England as cannot be said of our free country, that by law no labourer can be paid for labour in any other than lawful money. England holds any other payment to be a penal offence and punishable by fine and imprisonment. The same should be the case in every State in the American Union.

Under the mortgage system, no matter how industrious or economical the Negro may be, he finds himself at the end of the year in debt to the landlord, and from year to year he toils on and is tempted to try again and again, but seldom with any better result.

With this power over the Negro, this possession of his labour, you may easily see why the South sometimes makes a display of its liberality and brags that it does not want slavery back. It had the Negro's labour, heretofore for nothing, and now it has it for next to nothing and at the same time is freed from the obligation to take care of the young and the aged, the sick and the decrepit. There is not much virtue in all this, yet it is the ground of loud boasting.

ATTITUDE OF WHITE RACE TOWARDS NEGROES.

A NATIONAL PROBLEM.

I now come to the so-called, but mis-called "Negro

Problem," as a characterization of the relations existing in the Southern States.

I say at once, I do not admit the justice or propriety of this formula, as applied to the question before us. Words are things. They are certainly such in this case, since they give us a misnomer that is misleading and hence mischievous. It is a formula of Southern origin and has a strong bias against the Negro. It handicaps his cause with all the prejudice known to exist and anything to which he is a party. It has been accepted by the good people of the North, as I think, without proper thought and investigation. It is a crafty invention and is in every way worthy of its inventors.

It springs out of a desire to throw off just responsibility and to evade the performance of disagreeable but manifest duty. Its natural effect and purpose is to divert attention from the true issue now before the American people. It does this by holding up and pre-occupying the public mind with an issue entirely different from the real one in question. That which is really a great national problem and which ought to be so considered by the whole American people, dwarfs into a "Negro Problem." The device is not new. It is an old trick. It has been oft repeated and with a similar purpose and effect. For truth, it gives us falsehood. For innocence, it gives us guilt. It removes the burden of proof from the old master class and imposes it upon the Negro. It puts upon the race a work which belongs to the nation. It belongs to that craftiness often displayed by disputants who aim to make the worse appear the better reason. It gives bad names to good things and good names to bad things.

The Negro has often been the victim to this kind of low cunning. You may remember that during the late war, when the South fought for the perpetuity of slavery, it usually called the slaves "domestic servants," and slavery a "domestic institution." Harmless names, indeed, but the things they stood for were far from harmless.

The South has always known how to have a dog hanged by giving him a bad name. When it prefixed "Negro" to the national problem, it knew that the device would awaken and increase a deep-seated prejudice at once and that it would repel fair and candid investigation. As it stands, it implies that the Negro is the cause of whatever trouble there is in the South. In old slave times, when a little white child lost his temper, he was given a little whip and told to go and whip " Jim " or " Sal," and he thus regained his temper. The same is true to day on a large scale.

I repeat, and my contention is that this Negro problem formula lays the fault at the door of the Negro and removes it from the door of the white man, shields the guilty and blames the innocent, makes the Negro responsible, when it should so make the nation.

Now what the real problem is, we all ought to know. It is not a Negro problem, but in every sense a great national problem. It involves the question, whether after all our boasted civilization, our Declaration of Independence, our matchless Constitution, our sublime Christianity, our wise statesmanship, we as a people, possess virtue enough to solve this problem in accordance with wisdom and justice, and to the advantage of both races.

The marvel is that this old trick of misnaming things, so often displayed by Southern politicians, should have worked so well for the bad cause in which it is now employed ; for the American people have fallen in with the bad idea that this is a Negro problem, a question of the character of the Negro and not a question of the nation. It is still more surprising that the coloured press of the country, and some of our coloured orators, have made the same mistake, and still insist upon calling it a " Negro problem," or a race problem, for by race they mean the Negro race. Now, there is nothing the matter with the Negro, whatever ; he is all right. Learned or ignorant, he is all right. He is neither a lyncher, a mobocrat or an anarchist. He is now what he has ever been, a loyal, law-abiding, hard working and peaceable man ; so much so that men have thought him cowardly and spiritless. Had he been a turbulent anarchist he might indeed have been a troublesome problem, but he is not. To his reproach, it is sometimes said that any other people in the world would have invented some violent way in which to resent their wrongs. If this problem depended upon the character and conduct of the Negro there would be no problem to solve ; there would be no menace to the peace and good order of Southern Society. He makes no unlawful fight between labour and capital. That problem, which often makes the American people thoughtful, is not of his bringing, though he may some day be compelled to talk of this tremendous problem in common with other labourers.

He has as little to do with the cause of the Southern trouble as he has with its cure. There is no reason, therefore, in the world, why his name should be given to this problem. It is false, misleading and prejudicial, and, like all other falsehoods, must eventually come to naught.

I well remember, as others may remember, that this same old falsehood was employed and used against the Negro during the late war. He was then charged and stigmatized with being the cause of the war, on the principle that there would be no highway robbers if there were nobody on the road to be robbed. But as absurd as this pretence was, the colour prejudice of the country was stimulated by it and joined in the accusation, and the Negro had to bear the brunt of it.

Even at the North he was hated and hunted on account of it. In the great city of New York his houses were burned, his children were hunted down like wild beasts, and his people were murdered in the streets, all because "they were the cause of the war." Even the good and noble Mr. Lincoln, one of the best and most clear-sighted men that ever lived, once told a committee of Negroes, who waited upon him at Washington, that "they were the cause of the war."

Many were the men who, in their wrath and hate, accepted this theory, and wished the Negro in Africa, or in a hotter climate, as some do now.

There is nothing to which prejudice is not equal in the way of perverting the truth and inflaming the passions of men.

But call this problem what you may or will, the all-important question is: How can it be solved? How can the peace and tranquility of the South and of the country be secured and established?

There is nothing occult or mysterious about the answer to this question. Some things are to be kept in the mind when dealing with this subject and should never be forgotten. It should be remembered that, in the order of Divine Providence, the "man, who puts one end of a chain around the ankle of his fellow man, will find the other end around his own neck." And it is the same with a nation. Confirmation of this truth is as strong as proofs of holy writ. As we sow we shall reap, is a lesson that will be learned here as elsewhere. We tolerated slavery and it has cost us a million graves, and it may be that lawless murder now raging, if permitted to go on, may yet bring the red hand of vengeance, not only on the reverend head of age, and upon the heads of helpless women, but upon even the innocent babes in the cradle.

VII.

HOW THE PROBLEM IS SOLVED.

But how can this problem be solved? I will tell you how it cannot be solved. It cannot be solved by keeping the Negro poor, degraded, ignorant and half-starved, as I have shown is now being done in Southern States.

It cannot be solved by keeping back the wages of the labourer by fraud, as is now being done by the landlords of the South. It cannot be done by ballot-box stuffing, by falsifying election returns, or by confusing the Negro voter by cunning devices. It cannot be done by repealing all federal laws enacted to secure honest elections. It can, however, be done, and very easily done, for where there is a will there is a way.

Let the white people of the North and South conquer their prejudices.

Let the Northern press and pulpit proclaim the gospel of truth and justice against the war now being made upon the Negro.

Let the American people cultivate kindness and humanity.

Let the South abandon the system of mortgage labour and cease to make the Negro a pauper, by paying him dishonest scrip for his honest labour.

Let them give up the idea that they can be free while making the Negro a slave. Let them give up the idea that to degrade the coloured man is to elevate the white man. Let them cease putting new wine into old bottles, and mending old garments with new cloth.

They are not required to do much. They are only required to undo the evil they have done, in order to solve this problem.

In old times when it was asked, " How can we abolish slavery?" the answer was " Quit stealing."

The same is the solution of the race problem to-day. The whole thing can be done simply by no longer violating the amendment of the Constitution of the United States, and no longer evading the claims of justice. If this were done, there would be no Negro problem or national problem to vex the South or to vex the nation.

Let the organic law of the land be honestly sustained and obeyed. Let the political parties cease to palter in a. double sense, and live up to the noble declarations we find in their platforms. Let the statesmen of our country live up to their convictions. In the language of ex-Senator Ingalls: "Let the nation try justice and the problem will be solved."

Two hundred and twenty years ago the Negro was made a religious problem, one which gave our white forefathers about as much perplexity and annoyance as we now profess. At that time the problem was in respect of what relation a Negro sustains to the Christian Church, whether he was in fact a fit subject for baptism, and Dr. Godwin, a celebrated divine of his time, and one far in advance of his brethren, was at the pains of writing a book of two hundred pages or more, containing an elaborate argument to prove that it was not a sin in the sight of God to baptize a Negro.

His argument was very able, very learned, very long. Plain as the truth may seem, there were at that time very strong arguments against the position of the learned. divine.

As usual, it was not merely the baptism of the Negro that gave trouble, but it was as to what might follow such baptism. The sprinkling him with water was a very simple thing and easily gotten along with, but the slave-holders of that day saw in the innovation something more dangerous than cold water. They said that to baptize the Negro and make him a member of the Church of Christ was to make him an important person—in fact, to make him an heir of Jesus Christ. It was to give him a place at Lord's supper. It was to take him out of the category of heathenism and make it inconsistent to hold him a slave, for the Bible made only the heathen a proper subject for slavery.

These were formidable consequences, certainly, and it is not strange that the Christian slaveholders of that day viewed these consequences with immeasurable horror. It. was something more terrible and dangerous than the Civil Rights Bill and the Fourteenth and Fifteenth Amendments to our Constitution. It was a difficult thing, therefore, at that day to get the Negro into water.

Nevertheless, our learned doctor of divinity, like many of the same class in our day, was equal to the emergency. He was able to satisfy all important parties to the problem, except the Negro, and him it did not seem necessary to satisfy.

The doctor was a skilled dialectician. He could not only divide the word with skill, but he could divide the Negro into two parts. He argued that the Negro had a soul as well as a body, and insisted that while his body rightfully belonged to his master on earth, his soul belonged to his Master in heaven. By this convenient arrangement, somewhat metaphysical, to be sure, but entirely evangelical and logical, the problem of Negro baptism was solved.

But with the Negro in the case, as I have said, the argument was not entirely satisfactory. The operation was much like that by which the white man got the turkey and the Indian got the crow. When the Negro looked for his body, that belonged to his earthly master; when he looked around for his soul, that had been appropriated by his heavenly Master; and when he looked around for something that really belonged to himself, he found nothing but his shadow, and that vanished into the air, when he might most want it.

One thing, however, is to be noticed with satisfaction; it is this : something was gained to the cause of righteousness by this argument. It was a contribution to the cause of liberty. It was largely in favour of the Negro. It was a plain recognition of his manhood, and was calculated to set men to thinking that the Negro might have some other important rights, no less than the religious right to baptism.

Thus, with all its faults, we are compelled to give the pulpit the credit of furnishing the first important argument in favour of the religious character and manhood rights of the Negro.

Dr. Godwin was undoubtedly a good man. He wrote at a time of much moral darkness, and when property in man was nearly everywhere recognised as a rightful institution. He saw only a part of the truth. He saw that the Negro had a right to be baptized, but he could not all at once see that he had a primary and paramount right to himself.

But this was not the only problem slavery had in store for the Negro. Time and events brought another and it was this very important one: Can the Negro sustain the legal relation of a husband to a wife? Can he make a valid marriage contract in this Christian country?

This problem was solved by the same slaveholding authority, entirely against the Negro. Such a contract, it was argued, could only be binding upon men providentially enjoying the right to life, liberty, and the pursuit of happiness, and since the Negro is a slave and slavery a divine institution, legal marriage was wholly inconsistent with the institution of slavery.

When some of us at the North questioned the ethics of this conclusion, we were told to mind our business, and our Southern brethren asserted, as they assert now, that they alone are competent to manage this and all other questions relating to the Negro. In fact, there has been no end to the problems of some sort or other, involving the Negro in difficulty.

Can the Negro be a citizen? was the question of the Dred Scott decision. Can the Negro be educated? Can the Negro be induced to work for himself without a master? Can the Negro be a soldier? Time and events have answered these and all other like questions. We have among us Negroes who have taken the first prizes as scholars; those who have won distinction for courage and skill on the battle field; those who have taken rank as lawyers, doctors and ministers of the gospel; those who shine among men in every useful calling; and yet we are called a problem—a tremendous problem; a mountain of difficulty; a constant source of apprehension; a disturbing social force, threatening destruction to the holiest and best interests of society. I declare this statement concerning the Negro, whether by good Miss Willard, Bishop Haygood, Bishop Fitzgerald, ex-Governor Chamberlain, or by any and all others, as false and deeply injurious to the coloured citizens of the United States.

But, my friends, I must stop. Time and strength are not equal to the task before me. But could I be heard by this great nation, I would call to mind the sublime and glorious truths with which, at its birth, it saluted and startled a listening world. Its voice, then, was as the trump of an archangel, summoning hoary forms of oppression and time honoured tyranny, to judgment. Crowned heads heard it and shrieked. Toiling millions heard it and clapped their hands for joy. It announced the advent of a nation, based upon human brotherhood and the self-evident truths of liberty and equality. Its mission was the redemption of the wcrld from the bondage of ages. Apply these sublime and glorious truths to the situation now before you. Put away your race prejudice. Banish the idea that one class must rule over another. Recognize the fact that the rights of the humblest citizens are as worthy of protection as are those of the highest and your problem will be solved, and—whatever may be in store for you in the future, whether prosperity or adversity, whether you have foes without or foes within, whether there shall be peace or war—based upon the eternal principles of truth, justice and humanity, with no class having cause for complaint or grievance, your Republic will stand and flourish for ever.

FREDERICK DOUGLASS.

P D 17. 0.